LITTLE BOY JACK

Jane Landey

Copyright©2015

ISBN-13: 978-1522748410

Printed in U,S,A,

Grandparents

Grandparents raising grandchildren have received considerable attention in recent years.

Many observers perceive grandparent care to be a growing phenomenon. In fact, however, the proportion of children living with grandparents has remained relatively stable. Approximately 5 to 6 percent of grandchildren and 10 percent of grandparents

live in grandparent grand-
child households at any
given time. While these
percentages are low and
steady, in the context of a
growing youth population
they represent growing total
numbers. Nearly four
million children, and 1.5
million grandparents, live in
grandparent-grandchild
households.

These households face
unique challenges, which
vary depending on whether
the grandchildren's parents-
the middle generation are
also in the household.

Preface

A boy who was raised by his grandmother and who became alienated to his immediate family was Little boy Jack. The local industry that became the lineage work of a family was evidently a cooperation among a family set up. Jack, the little boy, who was the major character in the story was an obedient child succumbing to the order of his grandmother to join her in making a mountain out of a mole hill. His curiosity in the adventure activities of his father turned him into a fortune seeker and business magnate. The secret behind the tie and dye business which was forbidden by his grandmother to be revealed to anyone apart from Jack's immediate son paved way for the inquisitive of the employers and the unique success of it. It was noted also, the rapid growth and fame of this small industry. Killing two birds with one stone proved Jack to be an extra ordinary minded fellow, thus not Jack of all trades master of none but Jack of two trades and master of both. Thus the Little boy Jack turning out to be known as Powerful Jack.

Acknowledgements

The book, Little Boy Jack has references towards my maternal grandmother and her lineage. A woman of substance who gave unique doctrine to her children and grandchildren. Thanks go to all those who team up to organize the formation of this book.

Dedication

To my maternal grandmother,
Janet Loburo.

TABLE OF CONTENTS

Introduction

Native people used colors in a variety of ways. They used it in their ceremonies and their decorations, and to represent different aspects of nature. Yellow was made from sunflower and the roots of dandelions. Red was made from berries, red earth, a mixture of grey and yellow clays baked over ashes. Black was made from wild grapes, charcoals, and certain black earth. Some colors could be seen from greater distances than others. The colors used for their clothes were gotten from the barks of woods also.

CHAPTER ONE
Intruder

Jack was born on a wet day, his eyelids opened to a world full of bloom and scent of flowers. His grandmother carried him in her arms, rocking him by singing a lullaby. Little boy, little boy an intruder or a warrior. A royal king or a terrorist. Good one, you must choose little boy. Little boy Jack was christened after his grandfather, who in his youth was a great wrestler and ended up as a warrior. He had a royal blood and his next generation was prone to become a royal king. Grandfather and grandmother were parents of

Jack's father. Their compound was next to his father's smaller compound which comprised of three buildings and two shelters. The latter two were used as a kitchen and food storage. The little boy to his father was an intruder because he had taken up the affection dotted on him by his parents. Grandmother took up the care of Jack; put him on her back every moment except when he needed suckling. Jack's mother knew very about the growth of her son.

Dumping the bundle into the hands of her mother in law gave her all the freedom she needed. The little sibling put his right thumb in his mouth and sucked rapidly as if he had not been fed for days.

Grandmother was amazed to feel that the little boy, was not satisfied, who had just been fed. "Oh my little baby, soon mother will come. Do not worry." Jack began to grow under his grandmother's wing and not too long, his mother was pregnant, thus another child was on the way. This news gave grandmother total dominance over Jack. The growth of Jack was limited to the compound of his grandparents, despite the fact that his parent lived next door. Crawling around while grandmother engaged in her cloth dyeing.

She put the water in a big clay bowl far away from the crawling little boy's reach. Her hands were stained and she rubbed them on her cloth and swung the child on her back. She uttered no word and focused all her attention. This profession, tie and dye brought a huge income into the household. Grandfather depended on it, her son and family depended on it. Her two daughters who had been married to warriors from two villages came sometimes to demand financial assistance from them. Jack soon grew up as a young boy who helped his grandmother in her profession.

CHAPTER TWO
Playmates

Jack became a grown up boy who had many ideas to display. In the village of Toro, his limitation was the mid forest. His grandparents stopped him from going further, danger ahead, do not cross the palm trees," grandfather warned. One day, Jack and his village playmates went beyond the palm trees.

They went on hunting spree, which took hours before they could come out. It was a good hunting spree, a big deer crossed their path and with their spears and arrows, shot it down. The interior of the forest was so dark that they could not see clearly though many animals like squirrels, bush rats, birds were visible attractions. Jack wondered why grandpa would not want them to come this far. It must be the darkness or the way out, he thought. They did not know how they would find their way out at that moment. The four boys Jack, Wayo, Sede, Yuku, looked around and did one thing, threw a stone which they followed the direction. Carrying the big deer, two holding it by two hind legs and the other two holding it

by the forelegs walked carefully out of the thick forest. It took then hours to get out into the clear sky and by the time they got to the palm trees they were exhausted. They slumped down and took some rest. Afterward, they continued the walk back home. The evening was almost near and they must slaughter the animal and divide it accordingly. Arrival at Jack's compound was an explosion of noise from both parents and grandparents. "Where have you been since morning?" Grandfather demanded. "To the forest with my friends," Jack replied. "Where did you get this?" Papa asked. "It ran into our path and we killed it," replied Sede.

"You must have gone deep into the forest," expressed grandfather. "Yes, grandfather, out of curiosity," replied Jack. "They are becoming men, Papa," replied Jack's father. "Yes, I think they are," replied grandfather. "They are free now, I hope," said Jack's father. "Yes, they are free," replied grandfather.

The animal was skinned and divided into four. Each boy carried a share which they enjoyed for days with their families.

CHAPTER THREE
The Shed

Cooking was done in the shed, while the little children rallied round, watching as their mother stirred the sweet scented soup. The last of them whimpered, to signify urgency in the preparation. "My baby, soon, you will eat," mother said. Some food was served in a big pot and placed on a wooden tray. Mama called out to Jack, who ran in to carry the tray to his grandparents. If he was not around, Jack's sister, Elele, carried and seized the opportunity to greet her grandparents and enjoy some of the fat meat in the soup. "Have this, my child, it is good, your mother is a good cook," grandfather urged. She rushed back to eat her hot food. Mother had no other work to do apart from cooking and taking care of the children. She also tidied the house while the compound must be kept clean. The three girls trailed after their mother and helped her to clean by so doing, they were learning what they would do when they get married Jack was needed by her mother whenever she wanted some wood for cooking. How did he often get the wood? This was not a question to ask but who taught him.

Grandfather was responsible for his method of cutting down dry branches in nearby trees.

He taught him how to climb trees and cut down the branches without falling from the trees. Jack's little brothers and sisters knew little about him. They thought he was grandparents' last child. Therefore, they disregarded his ability to get closer to their parents.

Papa was very active in his work though he seldom stayed at home. People in his village saw him as someone who had no time for irrelevant things. The irrelevant things were those things other men admired doing most. These are getting together to drink or gossip together. He felt women were the full time gossips. No it was not like that in the village of Toro. The men had taken over this issue from women.

Papa concentrated on finding his treasures which he admired most. These treasures could be in the form of animals, birds or substances like, gold, iron, ore or herbal medicine. He came back with tangible treasure each time.

Little did Jack know about his father whom he saw occasionally. When he came home, he had much time with his grandparents and immediate family. During his visit to his grandparents, he took the opportunity to talk to him "How are you my boy?" He asked. "I am doing well Papa," replied Jack. "One of these days you will go with me to find treasure," he said to Jack ruffling his head. "Great papa," he said.

CHAPTER FOUR
Visiting

Jack visited the treasure forest with his father. He trotted along the zig-zag path. This was his first outing from Toro village to other villages. His father could only take him to a nearby village because he, was too young to travel long distance which he often embarked on. The first village, they explored was not as rich in treasure as other distant villages. They equally took something along from here. It was a tough herbal bark of a tree used for curing blindness. This would

bring much money for him after selling it to a knowledgeable medicine man. The tough herbal bark was hard to scrape off with the sharp machete. He took out of the bag, a sharp knife and with strong force pulled open the bark from the tree. He scraped off a long bark and folded it, tying it with a floppy string of a creepy plant. They moved on, digging and excavating to check what treasure lay beneath. They identified every object that came their way. Jack realized the importance of his father's work as a fortune seeker and treasure vendor. The next port of call was Jakara village where they slept on a flat branch of a tree. In the midst of a glowing fire which was made to scare off wild animals, Papa woke up in the night and patrolled round the forest. He embalmed his son in a tough aroma balm used to scare off animals in eating human beings or hurting them. He put on his head lamp and began to walk at close range of trees. Suddenly, he heard a movement, it was a leopard, though scared, he began to whisper softly, saying words taught him by his father. This words are used to transfix the animal for the killer to aim well at it. He brought out his arrow, which was already embalmed with poisonous oil. This would penetrate into the blood stream of the animal and weaken it. It worked magically, before long, the animal came closer and was about to jump, then he moved consecutively with his arrow. The leopard sprawled on the ground lifeless. He left the dead leopard and went back to his son. He slept little and not too long, the sun streamed in through the leaves of the trees surrounding them. Jack was astonished at the sight of the leopard that lay in front of him.

"Papa, how did you kill it? He asked?"

"It is the trick of the elders that I applied," he replied. They started the journey back to the village of Toro in good faith, one happy for the treasures they were taking back and the success of the activities, nobody was hurt. The leopard served many purposes, the skin would be sold to the king, who used it as a covering or carpet. The meat would be shared out to neighbors and friends including families. The teeth and nails would be used as medication by traditional medicine men.

They entered the village, from the outskirt to papa's compound; congratulatory messages were expressed by people they met.

CHAPTER FIVE
Jackpot

Jack took his jackpot and with his friends went to the meadows to play. The meadows were wet with the rain that fall two days ago. It had bought many birds flying in and singing on the wet trees. The usual four teamed friends gathered to enjoy the cool, clear and breezy weather. The yellow canaries flew across the trees, jumping on the branches and whistling joyously. They were alert, watching the kinds of birds to kill for their parents, especially the ones they loved most. The boys sat comfortably and watched expectantly for the swamp of birds which would make their mothers' soup very delicious. Suddenly, it happened, crowing of the forest birds were heard from a distance. They sprang to their feet and got their jackpots ready. Stones sharpened enough to knock down any of these big birds were placed in their jackpots. The birds arrived, like killing one stone with two birds, all they heard severally was, thud! thud! thud!. Each was able to bring down some of these giant birds.

They went home with the big birds and joyously gave them to their mothers. Jack's mother cooked it with melon vegetables. She pounded yam which they enjoyed with the soup. The following day, Jack's grandmother prepared a big pot for him to start his tie and dye. His big pot was placed on a tripod stand which enabled him to cook the dye and bring out the real color. This he used to dye the cloths. Jack began the task promptly, not only would he dye the cloths but also sew them into youthful styles and take them to the market to sell. Grandmother was happy that her grandson did not decline the offer. She quickly bought out the tied white cotton cloths for him to embark on. Helping grandmother was Jack's priority, not only would he get money out of it but he would experience a new life in the market. Jack had other things in mind, like becoming an adventurer like his father. He began to tie and dye cloths which he took to the market. Men and women began to buy them for their children, while some gave him extra money to make special wears for special occasions.

He was growing from a young boy to a young man who had already been granted a choice out of two professions. "I want to be like my father," Jack whispered.

CHAPTER SIX
Cloth Dying

Grandmother put a pot on the fire, filled it with water and allowed it to boil. It required a long time for such amount of dye to dissolve calmly without any lump left. The dyes were collected from the barks of special trees. The brown colors was collected from the hazel nut bark while the black color was collected from charcoal gotten from burnt wood. The red color was collected from another native tree. Nobody in the village knew the secret of where all the dyes were found.

Grandmother passed on the secret to her grandson and dared him not to tell anyone about it except his child. This was to be done after the child might have attained the same age in which she disclosed the secret to him. The sale of tie and dye had extended to the other surrounding villages. Jack had become a young man who was ripe for marriage at the moment. He carried his handwork to the market and surrounding villages. His handwork was appreciated by many and a lot of people bought them. He built a big shed in the market where some of the cloths were displayed. Thus Jack saw further advantages in grandmother's profession. He fancied doing it, though he had another profession which he really wanted to experience.

Tie and dye continued to flourish while grandmother counted the days she would hand over completely to her grandson. Jack on the other hand, started to explore the forest of Toro to look for the trees that fetched some other colors from the ones they had already known. One day, as he was putting together his local experiments some fruits on some native trees produced orange color as he added water to **it**. The tree was one of the giants trees and the fruits hung high up. The fruits must be ripe before they were used for this purpose He quickly acknowledged the trees by cutting deep, thus leaving a hollow which could identify the trees easily when he came round for the fruits.

Jack realized he had gained a lot from his grandmother and father.

On several occasion, he followed his father on different tips for adventures. His father's whole life depended on his adventures which had brought him wealth and fame. He went on special adventure when somebody sought medical aid or mineral ores. Sick people with chronic diseases who had been told by their physicians to drink cooked leaves of specific trees ran to him for help. Hurriedly, he embarked on a journey to where ever, these trees could be found. Combining cloth dyeing and fortune seeking was not welcomed by Jack. He waited for a day when he would hand it to his son as grandmother had advised. This would take a long time. Hopefully, he waited for such a moment. Thus, the swift beginning of a lineage of a profession inherited.

CHAPTER SEVEN
Clothes Of Many Colors

Grandmother washed the pot of dye, using a long broom. The inner part had become coated with different dyes and to prevent overlapping of these different colors on the cloths, she poured in some ashes and scrubbed the inside until it was clean enough to be used for further dyeing. She made a designed clothe of many colors which she sewed into a garment for Jack. He loved it and wore it many days. Jack's friend told their mothers to buy the same for them. Each mother came to grandmother and paid her some money to make similar clothes for their children.

One complained, "He did not eat last night, demanding I must buy the same garment for him before he eats in the house." Grandmother promised to make similar garments for them too. Few days after, theirs were ready too, in which all the boys put them on and patrolled the village showing themselves off. Soon, many parents visited grandmother and paid to her some money demanding similar garments for their children. She became a goddess among the children and Jack became an idol of fashion to reckon with at any time. He became somebody they looked up to for adventure and ideas.

The coat of many colors became a symbol of love and unity among children in the village. Whenever, there was a festival, grandmother made a uniform garments for the children and this fetched her a lot of money. People from other villages soon joined in buying clothes of many colors for their children. Grandmother began to make clothes of many colors in different designs and she seized to make only one color design. "Thanks to Jack who patrolled with the garment of many colors that I made for him," she said in admiration for Jack.

CHAPTER EIGHT
Outstanding

The family on the west wing of Toro village was seen as outstanding; one with unique nature and decency. Jack's family, ranging from his grandparents to his parents. There were other people in the village that had jobs as unique a Jack's family. Farmers played an important role in the village because they provided foods to the entire people. The planters of cotton could not have known how to spin it, while the spinner could not have known how to beautify it like Jack's grandmother. The physicians could not have cured his patients, if Jack's father had not assisted in bringing herbal medicine for them. The prescriptions of the physicians were the findings of Jack's father which he did not find difficult to get in any of his assessed forest. Jack was gaining popularity among his friends, who had taken to farming and hunting. Their lives were not as distinct as Jack, who had visited many villages and assessed many forests. He now occupied himself with finding more colors for his grandmother's profession, tie and dye.

Aro means tie and dye in Jack's language, soon the entire village and surrounding ones, began to call them Aro family. A name that spread beyond and people came in search of them. At last, a purpose was achieved and the outcome was extension of the dyeing work to those who wished to sell the finished work of the Aro family. Everybody in the family put all their effort to set on the customers' table different colors of cloths which they could use during different ceremonies. Their new inventions included, royal robes, bridal wears and new born babies ceremonial dresses.

The village of Toro became a colorful sight with the mode of dressing of the people. It was extended to other villages that had captured the same idea and vogue. Jack, eventually allowed his mother and sisters to dominate grandmother's work. They worked day and night while Grandmother and grandfather rested in the yard. It was over for grandmother and a starting point for mama and Elele, Jack's first sister. Breakfast, lunch and super were prepared by Sele and Erela who had learnt how to prepare delicious food from their mother.

When they were not preparing food, they helped mother and Elele with the tie and dye. Jack went into the forest to get fruits and barks to make dyes. He embarked on the special brands and prepared the finest dyes for the family work. Thus, the work grew into a giant one.

CHAPTER NINE
The Adventurer

Jack soon found himself on the path of fortune seeking and forests exploration like his father. There was no other work that could have fascinated him. He went beyond his father's adventure. His father had resigned from fortune seeking because of his age. He stayed at home and used the materials Jack brought from his adventure. There was much that had been done in a short while; those who did benefit praised the man who made such a thing possible. There were yet many things for Jack to put into place, such as getting bigger pots for the dyeing and having more time for his fortune seeking. He had to oversee the dyeing business and make sure the customers' needs were met. When he was not on expedition, he teamed up with his family and made sure he worked with them. His presence often increased the output needed to be sold.

Elele relied on the expert of his brother, who she felt had full knowledge on the work of dyeing. There were different patterns which Jack tied and they stood out fine after the dyeing process. Customers found it difficult to select at first sight since all were beautifully dyed. "This looks finer," said one customer. "No, I want the cool green and white design," said another customer. "Can I get more, my friends are also interested in buying ?" A woman inquired.

Jack made further experiment on what the dye could be used for and he came out with dyeing threads. Cloth weavers, weaved dyed threads into beautiful pattern, thick colorful attires were produced. Women bought them, tied one piece round their heads, another piece round the waist and the third piece, they placed on the shoulder. The woven cloths were also used to make shoes which were called Salubata. The men bought them and sewed caps and robes. They wore them on different occasions such as marriages, installation of a king or child naming ceremony.

CHAPTER TEN
Two Birds Worth A Million

Jack was faced with two birds worth a million and realized the rapid growth of the two heritages from his grandmother and father. Grandmother had become old and grandfather was too weak to do any heavy work. He became the sole proprietor of what he called a giant enterprise. More hands had joined the work of dyeing. The entrepreneur hired people to tie the cloths and some to dye them. A set of other people dyed thread for weavers to weave the prestigious colorful cloths. Little was known about the formula used in producing these dyes. Many workers who were employed sought how they could get hold of the method but all was in vain. Jack kept the secret and would not reveal it. The workers, who sought this out, often left, when they could not succeed in their plan. There was always replacement immediately. Many people were eager to work in the enterprise and got closer to the sweet smelling cloths.

Jack the little boy, had come to be known as "Powerful Jack". He had grown to a full young man, big, broad chest, and thick arms which went well with his tall height. He had fulfilled the desires of his grandmother and father. He still went on adventures which was his ambition, although the dyeing industry rested on his shoulders. He outweighed his friends at youth although their friendship had not diminished. They rather put their differences aside and all common factors were acknowledged. Jack gave gifts of dyed cloths and treasures to his childhood friends who he vowed to remain loyal to all the rest of his life.

They exchanged visits, ideas and products of their works. Thus Jack remained the brain behind "Aro cloth dying industry."

Epilogue

Jack thought over his past and how he became rich to help his friends. His advice to

them was, "Having all sufficiency in everything, you may have abundance for every good deed."

"For service as it fits your opportunities, and 'faith and beliefs'. First hold your head up high, and cut-out of the cycle of living in the workday rut!

Enough capacity means that: "You only need start with small (baby) steps toward having enough available, over time, for your goals and enough to give for helping your family and others in real need!

Then baby steps can grow toward building more *sufficiency* and to "*overflow*" (to give or share as you decide). Success is progress, and it is not too late to make progress, if there remains faith, charity and hope of your worthwhile life.

I learned how to see, I learned how to crawl, I practiced standing up, then I mastered the fall. I learned how to lie, and that

led to another, I learned how to apologize to my father and mother. I learned about the three R's, that was a

bore, though later in life I started craving them more. I learned how to run, first with legs apart, then I found out how falling down really feels. I learned how to fight, and got sick of defeat, I learned that this falling stuff is

where the road and rubber meet.

I learned that it was„ dog eat dog" and I wanted mine, and if I took the things I wanted "I" would be fine. Then one day, about a quarter-way through this game I thought I was standing tall, but was living in shame. I looked around me and no one was anywhere about I had fallen without knowing it; I was down and flat out.

With His help, we turned this way right, though the goal of a loving life was not yet in sight. I started on the inside, beginning deep within, hoping that I would find a natural smile again. I learned I could live, and wealth by my side, thanks – "It was a heck of a ride. I still fall, still getting better at it too. But I get up quicker, because I have got things to do. So if I could learn all that (and much more I didn't say) what can be accomplished now, even in a single day?

I learn to laugh at falls (after the effort, of course) we've got things to do– so we get back on the road.

Whether it's our work or our life –
yes, even our weakness. Stick to
your stance, you'll get through the
fog. You might fall, get bruised or
called out by the mobs, but
diamonds are lumps of coal that
stuck to their jobs. So as I get ready
for the second half, no more falling
(yeah, right)

I realize that great things are not
achieved by sudden flight. And
what of you, my friend and reader,
how's the trip on your road?
Remember, If you want the
rainbow, you have to put up with
the rain." Powerful Jack advised his
friends any time they gathered
during their social meetings.

Characters in the story

Jack
Grandmother
Grandfather
Father
Mother
Elele
Erela
Sele
Workers
Mothers
Jack's friends

Settings in the story

Toro village
Forest
Grandfather's house
Jack's home

Activities in the story

House work
Cloth dying
Selling
Hunting
Poaching
Herbal Medication

Names people called Jack in the
story.

Little baby
Little boy Jack
Powerful Jack

Local colors common for tying
cloth.

Black
Brown
Deep red
Grey

Other books by the author

Oddities in the House A
Season for love Teens
Crystal Memories
Return of the Slave Boy
Adventure of Couzan
Royal Crowns

Plays by the author

Pineapple
Destiny
Royal Crowns

Little Boy Jack
by
Jane Landey